Creative Freedom: The FWords anthology

Number

of a limited edition of 500 copies.

About FWords : Creative Freedom

'FWords' is a creative project to commemorate the Parliamentary Act of 1807 to abolish the British Slave Trade.

Eight individuals were selected from some of Yorkshire's most talented literary and visual artists, acclaimed through publication, performance, exhibitions and prizes, nationally, and in some cases, internationally. They were asked to respond to this occasion by focusing on the theme of Freedom.

FWords has been created to further raise the profile of Yorkshire's rich heritage of talented artists, descendants of those who migrated, forcefully and otherwise from Africa and beyond. In keeping with the theme, the writers and artists have been given as much creative freedom as possible to express their response to the commemoration which will ultimately be archived for Yorkshire's history. The work of six writers, has been illustrated with work from two visual artists, by creating printed materials, broadcasts, digital and dedicated web pages. All of these have been made free and accessible to the public.

The name, FWords was chosen as it was felt that within the concept of Freedom, there were so many ways and ideas to explain it, that it was not one that could be easily contained. The notions behind the word are both specific and nebulous, simple, but also complex, and as one of the writers says, in this sense, it is like love...

CREATIVE FREEDOM: THE FWORDS ANTHOLOGY

inscribe

PEEPAL TREE

First published in Great Britain in 2008
by Inscribe, an imprint of Peepal Tree Press
17 King's Avenue
Leeds LS6 1QS
UK

ISBN 9781845230739

'FWords' is an original signature project devised and funded by
Arts Council England, Yorkshire.

ARTS COUNCIL ENGLAND

For more information please visit
http://www.peepaltreepress.com/fwords/fwords.asp
www.facebook.com/people/FWords_Creative_Freedom/719177992
www.myspace.com/fwordscreativefreedom

Acknowledgements

The following pieces first appeared in *FWords: Creative Freedom* (Inscribe, 2007)

'Freedom' introduction by Caryl Phillips; 'How God Blessed Africa' and 'Hoe God Suid-Africa Seen' by Tanya Chan-Sam; 'Paradise' by Khadijah Ibrahiim; 'Surviving Freedom in Sunderland, April 2007' and 'Upon Opening Tina's 'Asylum Carwash'' by Jack Mapanje; 'AAAAAAAAAAAAAAAAAARGHHHH!' by Simon Murray; 'Sitting for The Mistress' by Seni Seneviratne; 'Full Moon' by Rommi Smith.

'After Qana – July 30th 2006' by Seni Seneviratne first appeared in *Wild Cinnamon and Winter Skin* (Peepal Tree Press, 2007)
'Tide' by Rommi Smith first appeared in *Dance the Guns to Silence: 100 Poems for Ken Saro-Wiwa* (Flipped Eye Publishing, 2005)

The artworks featured in this book were commissioned by Arts Council England, Yorkshire for the FWords: Creative Freedom Project in 2007:

Fosuwa Andoh, 'Paths to Freedom' Six Paintings
Olyseyi Ogunjobi, 'Flags for Freedom' Six Batiks

Cover design: liquoricefish
Cover photograph: Kadija Sesay
Photography of artwork: Glynis A. Neslen

CONTENTS

FREEDOM

Caryl Phillips

'Freedom' is, of course, one of those powerful words that suggests a different meaning depending upon who is speaking, who is listening, and where and when the word is being utilised. However, whether we are talking about India in the nineteen forties, or Ireland for most of the twentieth-century, or pre-Mandela South Africa, one thing is clear; the word carries *weight.*

A group of distinguished writers in the north of England in the early twenty-first century have been asked to respond to the word, and they have done so in a variety of forms. Their tones are both high and low, their pitch sometimes imploring, sometimes declarative, but their engagement is absolute. As one would expect, 'Freedom' means something different to each of these writers, but their elegant responses have in common an understanding that the word should be refracted through the prism of England.

Both Tanya Chan-Sam and Seni Seneviratne peer through an unrosy historical lens in order that we might see both pre-colonial and colonial history with a clarity which helps us understand the contemporary. The spiritual freedom and ecstasy of Khadijah Ibrahiim's work reminds us that England is no longer a place of cold concrete chapels, and religion is no longer to be shackled to dull hymns and draughty churches. There is 'Freedom' in belief, and English belief is no longer confined to Christianity.

The drama of Rommi Smith and Simon Murray's writing suggests connectivity to both love, and to a diasporan interpretation of self which works against the old, singular, notions of identity and belonging which continue to operate in England. The language they employ possesses a linguistic energy which is potent both in performance and on the page and, in this sense, their work neatly and powerfully transgresses canonically-inscribed ideas of what constitutes English poetry. In their very form, these writers are free.

Jack Mapanje sees a sad, almost melancholy, England behind the cold, modern, grimace. However, the country can also be warm and naïve, and his ability to render it with lyrical humour suggests a different type of freedom: *Knowledge* of this place. Perhaps this is the greatest freedom of all.

History is a story; a narrative which reaffirms the line of continuity along which people can trace their identity. Who belongs and who does not belong to 'England's concrete jungle'? The work of these writers demonstrates that not only do they belong, they also feel a powerful freedom to rewrite the story in a manner which makes sense to them.

Caryl Phillips
September 2007

Paths to Freedom
1/6 from a series of paintings **by Fosuwa Andoh**
'How God Blessed Africa'

Flags for Freedom
1/6 from a series of batiks **by Oluseyi Ogunjobi**
'How God Blessed Africa'

TANYA CHAN-SAM

How God Blessed Africa

London, 1836. Five men walk between the stone pillars of a government building on Whitehall. The front door swings open and a black suited usher welcomes them into an entrance hall. He leads them along a passage towards a staircase and pauses when one of the men stops to smell red blooms in a vase. Andries Stoffels, Cape Hottentot and Christian convert asks,

'What is these flowers?'

Dr Philip replies,

'Roses, Andries, these are roses. Come, we have no time.'

Andries wrinkles his nose as he smells the flowers and joins Dr Philip and the rest of their delegation who wait on the stairs. The usher nods his head and the group follow in silence up the stairs. At the top, he knocks on wooden double doors and leads them into a spacious high-ceilinged room. The Select Committee for Aborigines are seated around a rectangular oak table ready to hear the submission from the five men who represent a South African missionary delegation. Andries Stoffels and Dyani Tshatshu, both on their first visit to London, look around at the framed paintings on the walls and the blue velvet curtains that drape around the windows. They crane their necks to look at the mural on the ceiling and inhale the heady scents used by these leading members of London society. To one side of the room, three bespectacled clerks sit at smaller desks, sharpening pencils, filling ink pots and smoothing sheaves of paper. Two or three of the committee smoke pipes and the smoke drifts above the wooden dado rail. The chairman knocks on the brass ashtray to start the proceedings. He asks the head of the delegation, London Missionary Society envoy from the Cape, Dr John Philip, to read his statement. Dr Philip unpacks several scrolls of paper from a leather satchel. He speaks at length about the plight of the Hottentot and the

Xhosa at the Cape Colony. He talks fervently of the barbarism they face from the white settlers and of the Hottentot Code which offers the Hottentot but two choices; to become slave labour on the settler farms or to join the British Army. Their only salvation, says Dr Philip, is to join a mission station and become Christian. Only then will they be equal to the white settlers in the eyes of God.

'Slave, soldier or Christian,' mutters one of the committee, 'interesting choice.'

The chairman addresses the black man closest to him, 'Say your name for the record sir.'

Andries rises. The chair legs scrape under him and he turns in alarm at the sound. He feels certain the committee can hear the thud of his heart which sounds far louder than the trundle of hansom cab wheels on the road outside.

'Andries Stoffels, Christian, Gona Hottentot from the Cape…'

'Thank you Mr… Stoff…Stofferless. Tell me, although Dr Philip speaks highly of your people, there is still the question of the Frontier wars and the atrocities committed there. What do you think will change the unbelievers and warring factions to peaceful men and true Christians?'

Andries' breath huddles in his chest. He looks at the chairman and tries to recall the speech he practised with Dr Philip the night before. Like the shine rubbed into the polished wood beneath his fingertips, his rehearsed words seem to be rubbed from his memory. Andries' eyes jump from the chairman to the committee members as he searches for words in Gona, Xhosa and Dutch to translate into English, 'De Bybel charm us out of caves and from de tops of de mountains. De Bybel make us throw away all our old customs and practices, and we live now like civilise' men. Ik believe de only way to reconcile man to man is to instruct man in de truth of de Bybel.'

The chairman persists, 'What of the wars against the settlers? We read of the bloodshed at the Cape, the atrocities against innocent British settlers, women and children, who are forced to flee their farms because of the terror that the Xhosa and your people, wage on them.'

Andries clasps his hands together, 'It is true that our…that our…'

He squeezes his hands tighter. Dyani, seated next to him, leans forward and whispers, 'Ilizwe liyintombazana.'

Andries spreads his palms. He smiles, 'Ja, that's right,' his voice is louder, 'ilizwe liyintombazana.'

A movement at the clerks' desk stops him. They hold their quills aloft and look from one to the other with questioning expressions and confusion on their faces. It prompts Andries to say, 'I'm sorry, it mean, our country is still a young girl.'

His shoulders hunch close to his ears as he tries to draw breath past the sediment of anxiety on his chest, 'It is true, the Xhosa make war with de settlers. We, de Hottentot, have lost our lands and now because those of us who is Christian, we only want to serve de Lord…'

A committee members interrupts, 'There are still those of you who fight against the British, who attack the very mission stations. Why is this?'

Andries looks at Dr Philip, who keeps his head bent. He presses his fingertips into the table while he waits for Dr Philip to say something, like when they practised his speech and Dr Philip would say the next word and then he could remember the rest. He grinds his teeth trying to remember the next line but the words seem to have disappeared under the big river that runs through London. He swallows hard before he continues, 'Dis Hottentots and Xhosa people who fight, they ask for freedom and for dey land, because where we live… Freedom is not enough, dey want to mix land and water with de freedom, because den it is twentig times zoeter dan force and brutalness. But we have none land, none freedom and de only water is on de settler's farms, so what is left is de brutalness. But I believe, u Edelagbare, your Honour, we are God's chosen people because we were lost in our own land until de missions of Dr Vanderkemp came, Dr Read, and now Dr Philip. Until dey came, we did not know God, but I believe dat we can win dese battle with God on our side. We can change de unbelievers and evens de settlers. We, de Hottentot, have been saved. The Xhosa call us de people who have been brought to life by de word of God. Other peoples can also be brought to life, like us…'

Andries stands while the committee members make notes on their papers. The clerks leave gaps in the submission where Andries has used foreign words. The chairman checks that none of the other members have any further questions, 'Is there anything else you would like to add to your submission, Mr Stofferless?'

Andries looks up at the ornate ceiling with its carved cherubs and gilded cornices. 'We give thanks to Regina Victoria and the Aborigine Select Committee. We ask dat de British government give its Christian subjects freedom to live on our land again. It is written so; God said to Jacob, 'Dis land, which I gave to Abraham and Isaac, I will give to you and to your seed after you.' '

In the silence that follows, only the five petitioners bow their heads as Andries prays, 'Nkosi Sikelel' iAfrika.'

TANYA CHAN-SAM

Hoe God Suid Afrika Seën

Pretoria 2006. A man climbs the sandstone steps of the Union Buildings and walks down a passageway towards the West Wing. He keeps his head upright, swings his arms and looks straight ahead when he walks past the yellowwood office doors, polished to a magnificent colour and lit by the sun that shines through a double row of windows Once, he had an office here, as Minister of Law and Order. In those days, he bowed his head and obeyed the laws of his state and his god. He fought an eye for an eye and prayed for guidance from heaven in the fight against terror. In those days he signed order after order to ensure that the Black Cleric, whose office he was now heading for, could hardly walk after his torture. The Minister taps his chest to suppress an involuntary cough before he reaches the Cleric's door. Once he gains entry, he kneels on the new carpet, clasps his hands together in prayer and utters a sinner's plea to wash the Cleric's feet. In the minute's silence that follows, the Cleric looks down on the sinner's bowed head at the grey strands of hair covering the tips of the Minister's reddened ears. The Cleric searches his soul, his mind, his body for the grace of his god and lowers his hand onto the Minster's head. While the Cleric removes his socks and shoes, the Minister busies himself with arranging a towel on the carpeted floor, pours water from a flask into a steely grey bowl, while in his mind he translates his bible quote from Afrikaans to English before he says to the Cleric, 'Obey the Lord and He will heal the land.'

The seated Cleric nods in silent assent at the words of their common god and allows the Minister to guide his heels towards the bowl. The Cleric's delicate ankle bones twitch at the Minister's touch, in memory of a time, when he convulsed in near-death throes at a remote mission hospital, after an assassination order signed by this Minister to impregnate his underwear with toxic poisons. The Cleric's heel cupped in the Minister's palm break the water's surface as together they become submerged. The Cleric feels his chest tremble as he recalls the violent convulsions he fought during his illness. He regards his one-time would-be murderer and prays to his Lord for guidance to deliver this sinner from evil. On his knees, the Minister chants his scripture lesson, 'If I then, your Lord and Master, have washed your feet; ye also ought to wash one another's feet. For I have given you an example, that ye should do as I have done to you. Verily, verily, I say unto you, The servant is not greater than his Lord.'

The upturned hem of the Cleric's trousers touches the Minister's shirtsleeve. Above the hemline, the Minister witnesses a scroll of writing appear in the fabric. He turns his head to peer as silken colourful threads begin to convert the weave and stitch of the Cleric's trousers into beautiful script. Decipherable letters start to materialise into a list of names. The Minister searches for his own name in the heaven-sent vision. Before his eyes, the scroll undulates and begins to unravel. Stitches loop and kink in the fold of the cloth, unpicking themselves to form small nooses. Invisible needles sew threads which burrow and worm their way from the Cleric towards the Minister's shirt cuffs. He closes his eyes to stop them rolling and washes the Cleric's feet with fervour. As he cleanses his sins and his past, the threads spell out letters of the alphabet. First up one shirtsleeve, then the other. They write themselves onto his ironed collar, continue down his back, until finally, his whole suit of clothes is smothered in raised embroidered stitches. With his hands still underwater, the Minister snaps at the marching threads with his teeth. Soon his pockets are stuffed full of the tangled threads that spell out the names of the resurrected. They lie nestled among clots of blood, bones and severed fingers in fruit jars kept by police officers during the Minister's reign. Rampant stitches sew the missing bodies together, join lost handfuls of hair to bald patches and darn the future. Folded neatly inside his shirt pocket is his amnesty, stained and pierced by needle holes. One for each acknowledgement he gave to the thirty thousand lives he crushed. Because his countrymen and women dared to believe that they too were human and created equal in the image of his god. In his act of contrition, the Minister's tears drop into the waters below as his sins are released. He turns to the Cleric, 'We must obey the Lord and He will heal the land,' then bows his head and waits for his blessing. The Cleric lays his hand on this lamb that strayed from the flock, 'Thy sins are forgiven.'

The Minister lifts his face to the channel of God and inhales his first breath of freedom, 'Nkosi Sikelel' iAfrika.'

TANYA CHAN-SAM

Piss in the Bed

The wedding party was loud. Singing and dancing filled the yard outside. Neighbours from the surrounding farms sat on the stoep, and inside the house.

Sarah sat still on the bridal chair, decorated with offerings from her kinfolk. She kept her eyes downcast, as prompted by her mother. She'd been sitting for an hour; her bottom felt numb. The gaggle of conversation and laughter outside tormented her. She wanted to be outside, laughing with her cousins, sneaking a sip of beer. The mournful faces of the crying female relatives around her seemed strange and scary. She twisted a length of cream ribbon she'd pulled out of the hem of her dress. Her mother leaned over and grabbed it, bending down to rethread it through the hem. She said nothing but placed a firm hand on Sarah's knee, willing her to sit still. Sarah twined her fingers together, playing 'Duimpie, duimpie se maat...' silently to herself.

On a corner table, the wedding gifts were piled. Simple things like wooden spoons and farm produce wrapped in cloth, all illuminated by the paraffin lamp which had burned all day. Sarah swung her feet, trying to still the twitching in her legs. She'd heard so much about Meneer Jonkers, the farmer from across the valley. She knew he was older than she was but had never met him. Everyone said how rich he was. Her mother had told her he had running water inside his house.

Darkness arrived and with it Meneer Jonkers on his pony trap. The wedding party made two lines of back-slapping men and smiling women to hasten him to his new bride.

Sarah kept her eyes down, her heart racing, her fingers twined together, reciting in her head, 'Duimpie, duimpie se maat...' The wedding party was silenced by loud shushes from outside. Meneer Jonkers approached the bridal chair with care. He stood in front of Sarah, held out his hand to her. She placed her red knuckled hand on his;

his skin was like crepe, ridged with prominent blue veins. He led her to the table where the wedding meal was spread. Fatty mutton stew plumped out with vegetables cooked over the fires outside.

Meneer Jonkers was served first. He placed both elbows on the table and bent close over his steaming plate. His twitching nose and short eyelashes moved in his face as he absorbed the smells. Sarah watched him. Her mouth opened to mirror his, as he chewed the stewed meat. His chin, bobbing like a piston, drove his open-mouthed chewing. It reminded her of Oom Daan's old car, the engine guts laid bare, the pistons cranking up and down on their metal legs, devouring petrol and air.

Meneer Jonkers danced and sang on his wedding night. He clutched at Sarah, pressing his body into her breasts. She felt his hands push at her spine; his bearded jaw, tickled and pricked her flushed cheek. His voice, bass and hoarse, sang in her ear. He nuzzled at her hair. She heard him sniff. A sharp snort, up his nose. Sarah wondered if he could smell the Sunlight soap she'd bathed in. She tilted her head towards his nose, hoping he would smell the rosemary water her mother had rinsed her hair with.

Meneer Jonkers left with his new bride at cock-crow, the dawn sky bruised purple with new light. Their heads and shoulders were dark silhouettes as they clip-clopped away on his pony trap. His house lay across the valley, a journey she'd never made. True to her mother's words, he had running water in his house, a kitchen sink and bath in a bathroom. She followed him from room to room, open-mouthed.

In the kitchen he asked her to light the fire, fry meat and eggs. She busied herself, relieved to have something to do after sitting still for so long.

They ate alone at the large table. He ate again with gusto, grinning at her. Sarah finished her meal before him and played 'Duimpie, duimpie se maat…' under the table.

Finally he pushed his plate away.

'Wil Meneer tee he?' she asked.

He smiled at her and yawned. 'Ja, bring it to the room. I'm going to bed. Clean up the breakfast things, then come.'

Sarah busied herself, cleaning the kitchen, polishing the dusty, coal stove.

'Sarah, wat maak jy?' he called from the bedroom.

'Ek kom, Meneer,' she called.

She turned on the brass taps over the kitchen sink and water spouted out, warmed by the coal stove as he'd explained to her. She washed the two plates, holding out her hand in delight under the running water. Turned off the taps and started again.

'Sarah, wat maak jy?' he repeated from the bedroom.

'Ek kom, Meneer,' she called.

She searched for cups and saucers, a tray, sugar basin. Arranged them on the tray, covered with a beaded doily she found in a drawer filled with cloths and doilies. One for each day of the week. She traced her fingers over the neat embroidery. Recognised 'Sondag' from the same letters she'd practised in Sunday school.

'Sarah, waar is jy?'

'Ek kom, Meneer.'

She tested the water in the copper kettle. She wondered if it was hot enough to be carried down the long passage to his bedroom. She'd never had to transport tea before. Surely the air would cool it and Meneer Jonkers would not want a cold cup of tea. Back on the centre hot plate she moved the copper kettle. It had to be singing, her mother had said.

'Ek kom, Meneer,' she called before he asked again.

Every step down the passageway was carefully placed, her eyes wide, her hands gripping the tray, holding it tightly. Another few more steps. Not a drop spilled.

The door swung open. Meneer Jonkers stood on the threshold. Bare-arsed naked. Poedel-nakend. She must have fainted. The tray must have fallen. Meneer Jonkers must have tried to catch it and the hot-hot tea must have fallen on him. Spilt over his pancake-flesh skin, the sparse grey chest-hairs turning orange as the hot, dark tea emptied onto him. His heart in his frail body must not have been able to withstand the shock.

Sarah arrived sweating and barefoot at her old home, her wedding dress dirty, the ribbon dangling around her knees.

'When I found him he was poedel-nakend and dead. The Lord knows how it happened. The Lord only knows!' she shouted at her bleary-eyed mother.

The news must have grown wings, flew over the whole valley that morning, because by mid-afternoon, their stoep was again full of Jonkers' relatives, looking solemn and in no mood for festivities.

'A charge must be laid.'

The Jonkers family nodded their heads in agreement. Their relative had to have justice.

Three months later in the District Circuit Court, held in the town hall, Sarah sat on the wooden chair she had been escorted to. She could hear the sounds of bodies moving behind her as the public filed in, heard the low hiss and murmur of dress fabrics and trouser material as thighs and bums sat down, the twisting of arms and backs as coats and jackets were removed. Sarah could hear whispered voices, low greetings and someone laughing. A voice called out for the windows to be opened, to let in fresh air. The clerk rose from his seat. Sarah's head turned as her eyes followed him walking towards the tall windows of the town hall. A row of Jonkers relatives met her gaze. A clump of them reared in unison, shouting, 'Moordenaares!'

Sarah turned in panic, searching the rows of faces for her mother. She found her sitting upright in the middle of a row of female relatives, all dressed in black, staring ahead.

Sarah twisted back in her seat, placed her palms on her knees to stop them shaking. From the back of the court room, a rumble of voices replied to the Jonkers family's outburst.

'She's bleddy wel innocent!'

'Sarah Jonkers is a tragic young bride widowed the morning after her wedding. Have some pity!'

Sarah looked ahead, where the judge's table stood, the chair fitted neatly under the table, awaiting him. She kept her wide eyes on the judge's empty seat, twisting her fingers around themselves, quietly whispering, 'Duimpie, duimpie se maat, langeraat, fielafooi, pis innie kooi.'

Paths to Freedom
2/6 from a series of paintings **by Fosuwa Andoh**
'Paradise'

Flags for Freedom
2/6 from a series of batiks **by Oluseyi Ogunjobi**
'Paradise'

KHADIJAH IBRAHIIM

Paradise

اَلنُّوْرُ

Imagine *An-Noor*,
The Light from beyond the sky,
flying over England's concrete shore
to straighten the curve in your back,
remove the screw in your face –
signs of centuries of loss and pain.

اَلنُّوْرُ

Imagine *An-Noor*,
African dust between your toes
motes rising
as you walk in a circle through
soft sand and sea,
in the cool night air before the white
thread of the dawn is lifted.
Paradise lies at the feet of your mother.

اَلنُّوْرُ

Imagine *An-Noor*
in a Sufi chanting,
polished ebony with the grace of an angel,
body entwined
in white and indigo *njaxas* cloth,
swaying from side to side
in order
in time;
Ar-Rahman, *Ar-Raheem*, *Al-Kareem.*

اَلنُّوْرُ

An-Noor is what you see
within the stars and the moon,

all regal and auspicious,
in *dhikr* you meet the morning sky;
finger tips turn *tasbih* beads;
delicate hums cascade
like silken sheets,
soften the heart.

Enter a place where time has
not damaged the heart,
freedom in motion;
Ar-Rahman Ar-Raheem, Al-Kareem,
All Merciful and Beneficial,
99 names – softly, in harmony.

اَلنُّوْرُ
Imagine *An-Noor*
fusing tales of separation,
cut from Atlantic's ocean bed
and a Sufi chanting, whispering Allah's name;
Ar-Rahman, Ar-Raheem, Al-Kareem,
99 names – softly, in harmony.

A Sufi chanting,
and paradise lies at the feet of your mother,
straightens the curve in your back,
removes the screw in your face,
keeps African dust rooted between your toes.

اَلنُّوْرُ
Ar-Rahman Ar-Raheem, Al-Kareem, An-Noor

Note: Muslims (particularly Sufis) teach that there are 99 names for God, *An-Noor* – is one of the names, which means 'The Light' in Arabic – (light / guide to freedom).

Dhikr – remembrance – to be in a state of remembrance of God – free from everyday surroundings – a sense of paradise.

Njaxas – patchwork cloth (in the Wolof language) – often indigo and white.

Tasbih – prayer beads.

KHADIJAH IBRAHIIM
Dancehall Sound Clash

I reminisce on heartical times
when Sir Coxson did rub-a-dub
with cool vibes, an' Saxon
toast bonafide bionic rhymes.

I reminisce dancehall 1980's style
with an exodus of speaker boxes
in old vans ready to line walls
at Chapeltown Community Centre,

where wires spiral through soundman hands,
connect dread man at de control
with turntable, amplifier and tweeter
an selected sounds of Mama Africa's sons:

Marley, Tosh, D Brown, Jacob Miller,
Jamrock raw roots reggae riddims:
Do you know what it means to have a revolution?
Fighting against downpression.

In the height of sound clash
Manchester and Leeds strike a match
Baron high power came to test tunes
Sparta sound boy head dem swell.

In London King Tubby came too,
dropped dub plates inna de dance.
But Jungle Warrior crew got fresh,
with a deeper cylinder-charge in the bass-line.

Revolutionary sounds of rasta
weaved through head wraps,
beaver hats, red, gold and green tams,
and dreams of the promised land.

Irie skanking lean foot youths
in Clarks' heels and Bally brand boots,
Sistrens in pencil pleated skirts,
armed with passion eena rub a dub dance,

lick wood, praise Jah, summons
order to selecta fe *Lift it up,*
pull it back, come again.
In dis I and I reminisce.

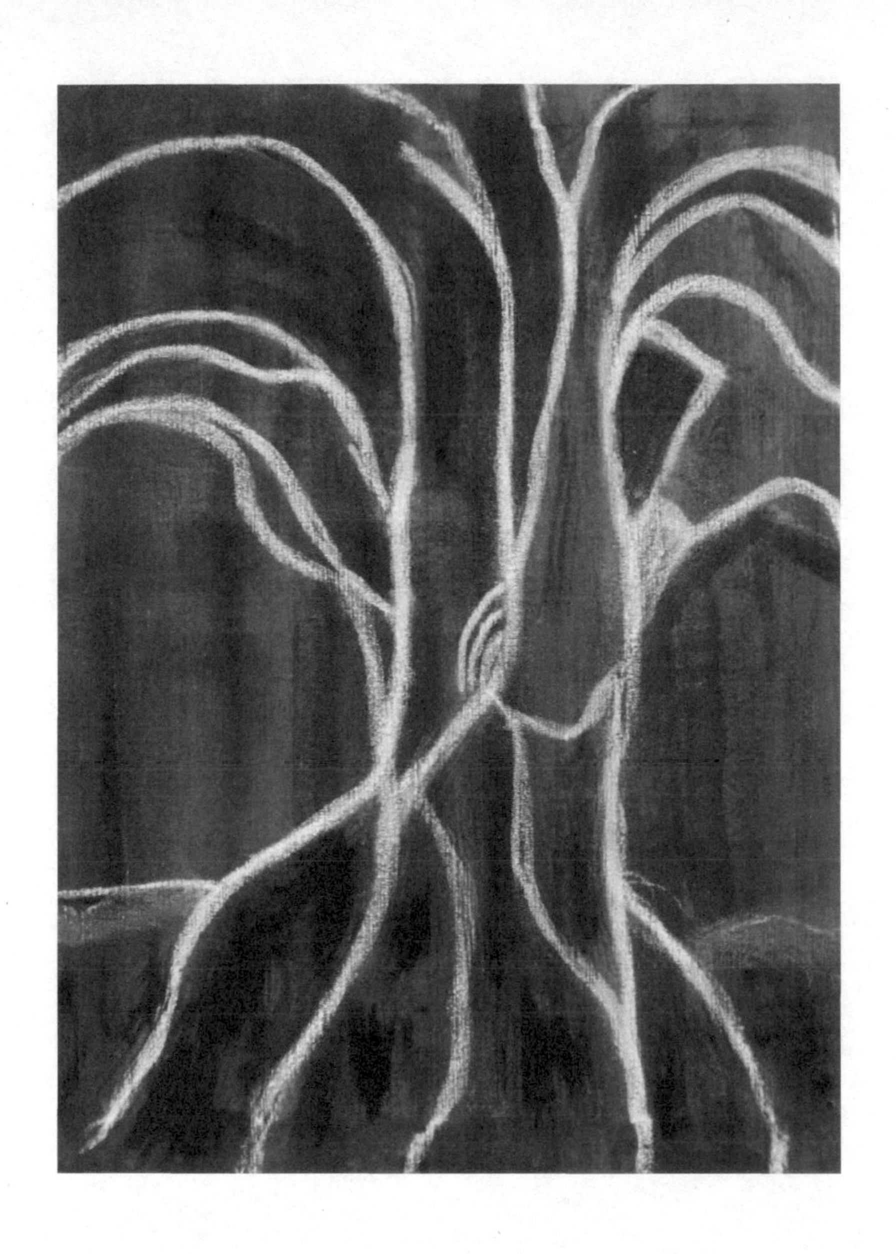

Paths to Freedom
3/6 from a series of paintings **by Fosuwa Andoh**
'Surviving Freedom in Sunderland, April 2007'

Flags for Freedom
3/6 from a series of batiks **by Oluseyi Ogunjobi**
'Surviving Freedom in Sunderland, April 2007'

JACK MAPANJE

Surviving Freedom in Sunderland, April 2007

And should the traffic police disrupt
your direct route from A19 because
another truck has shed its load in front
of you; should your diverted traffic
snail tediously past toughened faces
of villages struggling to rescue their
dignity after long lost coal and ship-
building industries; should you lose
your way zig-zagging and criss-crossing
the city's maze of cul-de-sacs, one-way
streets, weird roundabouts and green,
grey and other bridges; should you
begin to panic about your delay and
the petrol running out –
                                        Do not frighten
the senior citizens unravelling the lyrics
of their seagulls flying over the seafront
nor interrupt the Empire Theatre box
office girls forever chattering on line;
just take on the city's three old ladies
at the nearby bus stop, they'll show you
The Green Terrace campus, precisely
where your audience is waiting to hear,
gratis, how you survive your liberation.

JACK MAPANJE

Upon Opening Tina's 'Asylum Carwash'

I

Opening Tina's 'Asylum Carwash' project
At Sunderland Museum & Winter Gardens
The other night was the easiest part; you
Needed only to cite the slave trade abolition
Bicentenary and invoke the composer of
'Amazing Grace' that the globe reveres –
More than the slaves he brutalised before
He suitably repented – and the job's done.
The toughest part
Must have been for Tina Gharavi and her
Mates to convince South Shields refugees,
Asylum seekers and other minorities who
Create carwashes out of nothing to thrive,
That this too was another worthy venture,
To help them pay their dues to Caesar and
Survive the harsh elements they encounter
Every North East Winter.

II

Introducing the eight hour documentary
That is meaningful without a story, script
Or words, to Arts Council and other patrons
Of slavery abolition schemes in Sunderland
Museum & Winter Gardens the other night

Was the lightest of duties; you needed only
To read our hypocritical societies in the actors'
Car hot wash, the soaping, waxing, rinsing
And drying – no rollers, no brushes – just
God's own perfect hands, to spot the slavery.
                                        The hardest part must
Have been for Tina Gharavi to sway her
Creators to Sunderland Museum & Winter
Gardens, to mingle nervously with their
Patrons, sampling samosas, sandwiches
And other civilised nibbles, washing them
Down, not with red wine or beer, but with
White wine, juices and sparkling water.

III

Speaking at the 'Asylum Carwash' Exhibition
In Sunderland Museum & Winter Gardens
The other night was the least painful duty; you
Needed only to meet the actors and creators
On their own terms, to appreciate their magic
In gathering their dues to Caesar and thriving;
                                        The greatest challenge for all:
Directors, actors, patrons, you and me must
Surely be, as we wish the project's country
Tour well, whether we are listening or merely
Taking 'Asylum Carwash' as another 'Amazing
Grace' in the atlas of our abolition of slaveries!

JACK MAPANJE

The Cost of Impotence

(For Blaise Machila)

How do you thank a colleague who
sets himself the task of finding out
on behalf of your distraught family
where security officers have dumped
you after ferociously abducting you
leaving hearts throbbing with fear?

How do you treat the brother's scars
after months of torture in police cells,
when one day the security officers
should drag him into your prison,
leg-irons, hand-cuffs and all – to stay
caged throughout his incarceration
as instructed by his college principal?

And when his mental state worsens,
what do you do when your mate casts
off the foya he was forced to wear on
arrival, the blanket rags he preferred
and, to everybody's horror, decides
to do his time totally naked – refusing
to speak even to you, his only friend?

What do you do after your appeal
for Vice Chancellor to come and see
the state of mind of his scholar, before
he makes his final approach for His
Excellency the Life President to have
compassion on your friend; how do

you face your comrade when, utterly
mad, he should chuck out the very
VC intending to rescue him, of course,
hoping against hope that he'd visit
you too, surreptitiously – though as
for that, what a nightmare botched!

No, Chancellor College principal, no,
your uncle and chairman of university
council, no, your sister, life president's
permanent mistress and official hostess,
the mama – how could you unleash
your power on such culpable people?

And what homes, what families, what
lives – indeed what husbands, wives,
children, what lives, dislodged, disrupted,
scattered, what pain inflicted forever!
When will you learn there's no need
to assault the people you want to rule?

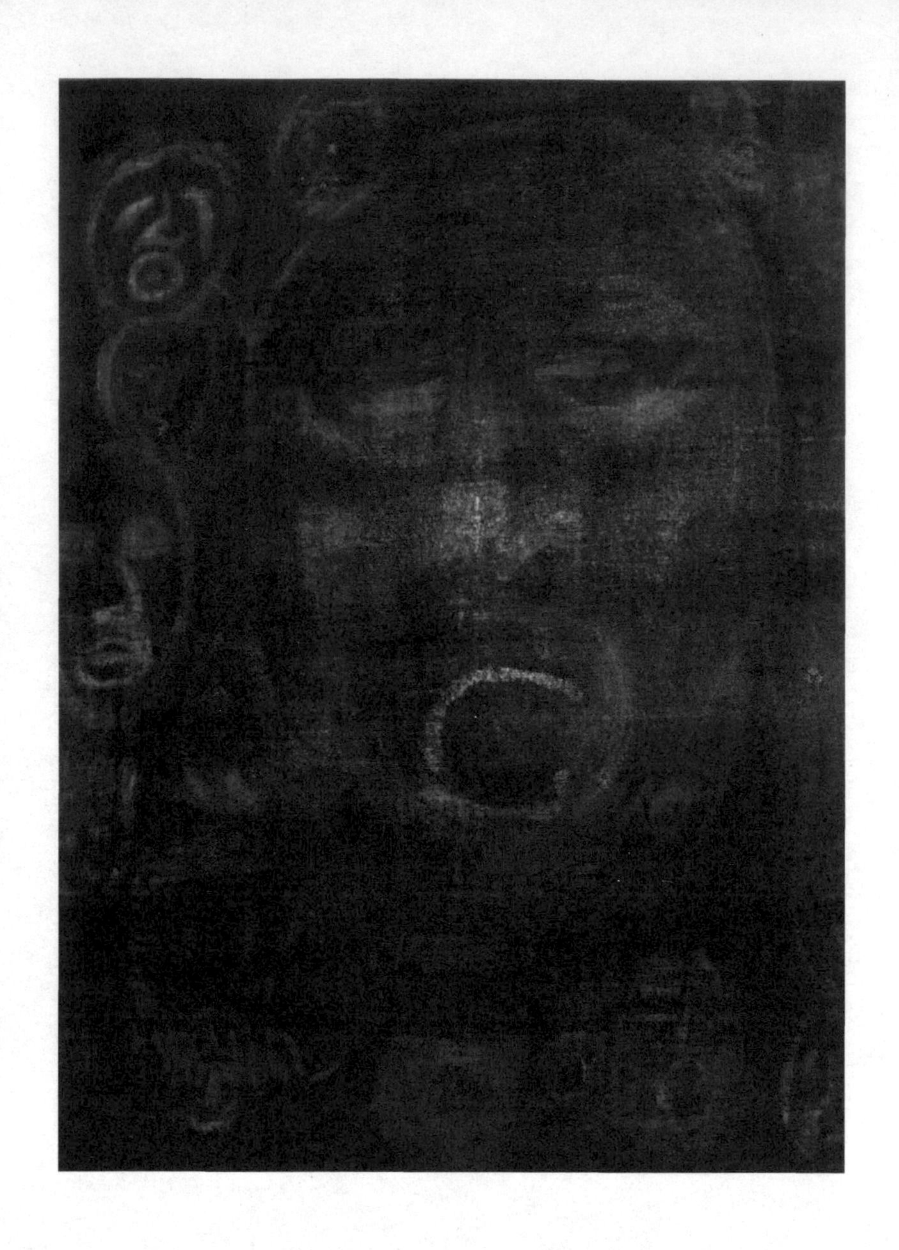

Paths to Freedom
4/6 from a series of paintings **by Fosuwa Andoh**
'AAAAAAAAAAAAAAAAAAARGHHHH!'

Flags for Freedom
4/6 from a series of batiks **by Oluseyi Ogunjobi**
'*AAAAAAAAAAAAAAAAAAARGHHHH!*'

SIMON MURRAY

AAAAAAAAAAAAAAAAAAARGHHHH!

AAAAAAAAAAAAAAAAAAArghhhh!---
---bolish all
celebration, commotion,
promotion of the notion
that we are free,
de owner of de plantation ∞
now owns de penitentiary

I hear voices:

A chemical brown voice
blairs out
from behind
a plastic bush:

ASBO
TESCO
GITMO
LET'S GO
BACK TO WORK
BACK TO SCHOOL
NO STOPPING
BUSINESS AS USUAL
– CARRY ON SHOPPING.

Organic green voice
spreads seeds
like
neglected weeds:

aaaaaaaaaaA-bolish all
co-operation with corporations,
i-pod, i-phone, i-home, i-clone,
i, i, i… me, me, me, me, me,
quicker cheaper contracts
cannot bring liberty,
turn off big brother,
see reality c--c--t--v
de owner of de plantation ∞
spells apartheID with ID…

Chemical brown
blairs out
from behind
plastic bush:

HUMAN RIGHTS
HAVE GONE WRONG
POLITICAL MADNESS
HAS GONE CORRECT
SEVEN SEVEN
NINE ELEVEN
DATES WE CANNOT
EASILY FORGET.

Organic green
spreads seeds
like
neglected weeds:

aaaaaaaaaaA-bolish
abomination
of a bomb-making nation.
erase email,
turn facebook face to a book,
reclaim time and space
that myspace took,
look up from the gutter,
dim stars of celebrity,
the owner of de plantation ∞
CEO of military…

brown blairs
behind chemical bush:

FREE PRESS
FREE VOTE
FREE MARKET
FREE TRADE
EVERYTHING UNDER CONTROL
DON'T ASK WHERE –
OR HOW – IT'S MADE.

green spreads weeds
neglected seeds:

aaaaaaaaaaA-bolish de myth
of freedom granted
by philanthropist
free freedom fighting names
of CLR James,
Nkrumah, Nanny, Nehanda and a

thousand Dessalines;
stitch bullet-holes of history
and herstory to see
de owner of de plantation ∞
media monopoly…

brown blairs behind bush:

STICK TO THE CURRICULUM
STAY ON COURSE
TURN TO THE CHAPTER
'ABOLITION
= WILBERFORCE'.
DO NOT UPSET THE SPONSORS
NO, IT'S NOT HYPOCRITICAL
FEEL FREE TO SPEAK FREELY
JUST MAKE SURE IT'S NOT
PO-LIT-I-CAL.

green weeds spread seeds:

aaaaaaaaaaA-bolish
media monopoly, ID, military,
abolish bomb-making nations,
abolish corporations,
abolish the penitentiary
and – to be truly free,
abolish plantation owners
of de e-k-k-k-onomy.

SIMON MURRAY

A Bad Grain Of Rice

I hated my Dad.

I'm sure all kids at one time or another hate their parents: those times when they are punished; when they are denied freedom; when they are denied the 'new-must-have-latest!' toy/ fast food/ experience that everyone else has got, has eaten or has visited. I did not hate my Dad because he rationed my sugar addiction. I did not hate my Dad because he attempted to counter the billion dollar advertising industry's seduction of my tiny mind. I certainly did not hate him because he beat me or abused me (he was a loving, caring father who did neither). No, I hated my Dad because he was Black.

We lived in a White neighbourhood. My brother and I, two Sri Lankan brothers up the street and a brown-skinned boy (of parentage I never discovered), all went to a White school. All my teachers were White. All the people who went to the playschool, cub-scouts, church and Sunday school that I was required to attend were White. All my closest friends were White. My Mother was White.

My Dad was Black.

I hated my Dad because his presence at the school gates, at parent's evening and at sport's days reminded me that I was not White. I remember shrinking down into my parka-coat, shirking away from his proud, beaming Black face. He was so obvious; no thoughts for my embarrassment. He would even chat to the other parents with no shame. I could feel other kids staring at him, staring at me, placing us together, wondering, marvelling. Who's that? Is that his Dad? That's his *Dad*? Look how *Black* he is. He stood out amongst all the normal White faces. A bad grain of rice in the dish. He spoiled everything.

Many years of Grade A education naturally did nothing to instil any pride in my Caribbean and Afrikan heritage and so my journey towards being proud of my Dad, being proud of who I am, and knowing who I am, has been a long and continuing extra-curricular activity. It is a journey which began with valuing the acceptance of friends and society over the acceptance of who I was. A journey that included the lowlight described above, as well as all-too-familiar incidents of name-calling, taunts, patronising pats of my afro, scuffles, fights, and even the self-application of a clothes peg to reduce the size of my nose.

It was left to my patient parents to see me through this period of society-induced self-hate – my parents, together with Viv Richards, Malcolm Marshall, Frank Bruno, Daley Thompson, Ben Johnson, Prince, Michael Jackson, Bob Marley, John Barnes...

Several trips to Barbados, the island of my father's birth were also a great help and I slowly began to love difference: I came to love different hair, different food, different music, different talk, different customs, different culture, different society, different land, different history...

Today, my journey has led me to understand that race is an illusion – a social construct that has no basis in scientific fact. We are all one race. All people come from two parents. All people who come from two parents have two heritages and two cultures from which they are formed. All people are mixed-heritage. I am simply blessed and have the advantage of being been born into a family that was made by the union of two people from two apparently differing cultures.

I am not mixed-race.

I am not Black or Black British: Black African, Black Caribbean or Any other Black background.

I am not Asian or Asian British: Asian Bangladeshi, Asian Indian, Asian Pakistani or Any other Asian background.

I am not White: British, Irish or Any other White background.

I am not Chinese.

I am not Asian and White.

I am not Black African and White.

I am not Black Caribbean and White.

I am not Chinese and White.

I am not Any other background from more than one ethnic group.

I am not Any other ethnic group.

I would prefer not to mark a box to describe my background.

I would prefer that this information was not used for monitoring purposes.

I am not 'other'.

I am proud of who I am and where I come from. I feel nothing but respect and pride for the courage and dignity shown by my father in overcoming the deep-seated prejudice, racism and all the deliberate obstacles put in his way to stop him earning the acceptance and the high community-standing he now enjoys.

I am who I say I am depending on who is asking, depending on what the question is, depending on what my mood is, depending on how the question is asked and why the question is asked.

Today I am a Pomfretian-born Yorkshire writer of Bajan heritage. Tomorrow I may be an artist, poet, designer, gardener, cook, teacher, student, handyman, lover. The day after I may choose to define myself as a revolutionary internationalist Pan-Afrikan anarchist activist. Or not.

I am who I choose to be. An Afrikan. A human being. Homo Sapiens. Male.

I love my Mother. I love my Father. I'm cool with my wide nose.

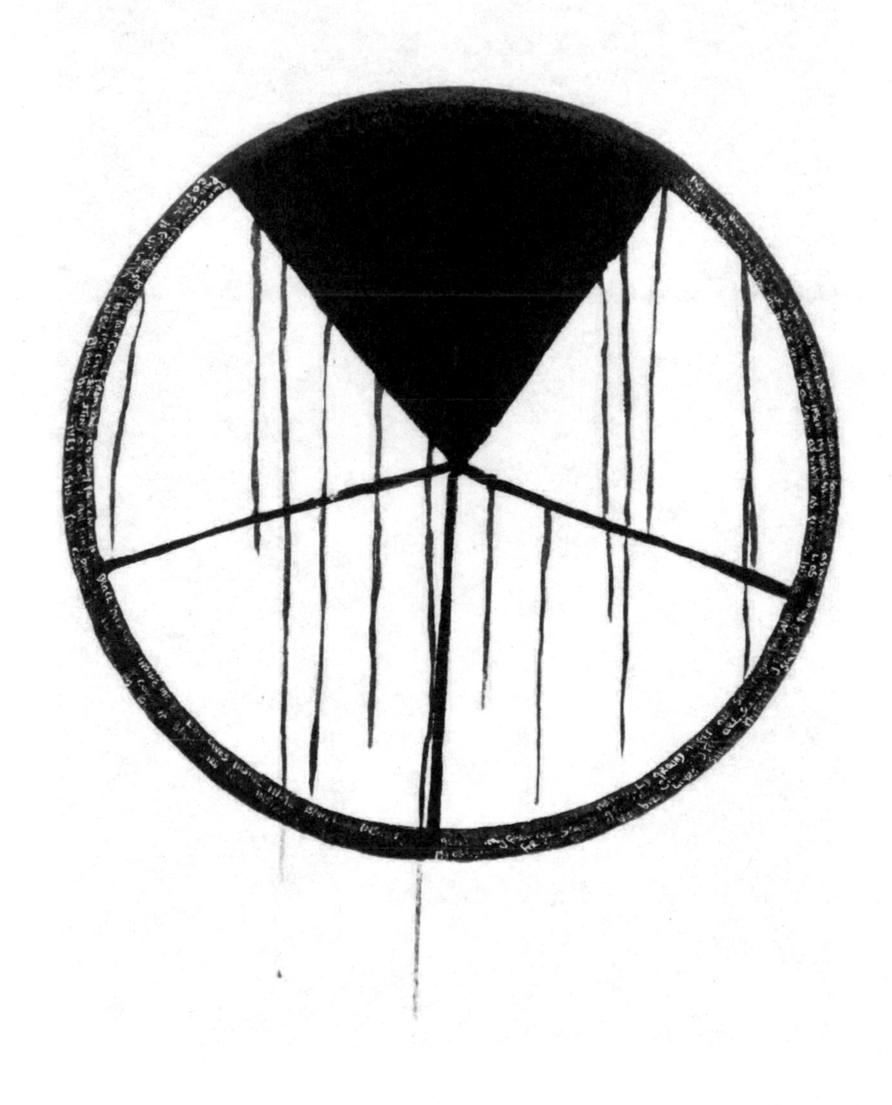

Paths to Freedom
5/6 from a series of paintings **by Fosuwa Andoh**
'Sitting for The Mistress'

Flags for Freedom
5/6 from a series of batiks **by Oluseyi Ogunjobi**
'Sitting for The Mistress'

SENI SENEVIRATNE

Sitting for The Mistress

Detail from a portrait of French aristocrat, Louise de Kéroualle, Duchess of Portsmouth, a mistress of Charles II, posing with her black child servant. Oil on canvas, Pierre Mignard, 1682.

First sitting

Blackbird lives inside me and the mistress
knows. She calls me her *petite merlette*
and tells me I mustn't worry because
inside my black skin is a soul as white as
the pearls she has tied so tight around my neck.

She says I was three when she washed the devil
away. My head pushed back, water swamped
my face so I couldn't breathe. She says if I do
bad things I'll make it black again. Then she'll
have to clip her little blackbird's wings.

The mistress says I must stand beside her while
Monsieur Mignard makes us up with colours that
smell; that we will be a painting, in a gilded frame,
hanging in the halls of the Palace of Whitehall;
that the King will be pleased; that her skin will be

lead white, against the burnt umber and lamp-black
of my skin. My head spins and Monsieur shouts,
Look at the mistress, not me! Tilt your chin up!
I gaze at her neck. The collar of pearls stifles mine.
I try to see her soul inside her skin.

Second sitting

Blackbird lives inside me.
There are feathers everywhere.
I sweep them into small piles, far down
below my ribs and smile like the mistress tells me.
Parched lips stretch across dry teeth and pull my cheeks.

As if cheeks would melt. The face very close
in my dream squeezing mine as if our cheeks
would melt into each other. Tears trickling
over me and the mouth kissing.
Blackbird stirs and the feathers blow.

They clog my throat. When I cough out
feathers, the mistress laughs, asks why
I bark like one of the King's spaniels.
Merlette aboye comme un chien.
Blackbird takes flight.

One swoop, two swoops, three swoops.
My feet are scavenging for solid ground.
The mistress will be angry. Behind her head
One… two… three clouds in a painted sky
slow me… one…two…three…down…

Third sitting

Blackbird lives inside me.
She sleeps while Monsieur Mignard
mixes colours in his pots of clay.
My hand is too small for the weight
of this pearl-filled nautilus shell.

If I tremble, if the shell tips over,
if the polished pearls fall, the mistress
will be angry. One red jewel, two red jewels
three red jewels dripping from her dress.
Blackbird shifts.

The mistress rests her arm across my back.
So light a touch, a tickle on my shoulder.
A touch, a lift, a strong arm round my legs,
a hand cupped under my armpit, fingers
pressing on my back. Blackbird flutters,

I gulp feathers. Heavy eyes count blackbird
back to sleep. One … red … jewel … two…red
jewels … three … red… Mistress nips my shoulder.
Look at me and smile, merlette!
You will spoil the picture!

Fourth sitting

Blackbird lives inside me. She is learning
to be still. She watches Monsieur Mignard
as he watches me. The crimson coral chafes
my fingers, rough like the blanket that we
hide under at night, in the damp room that

smells of the big grey water, licking the palace
walls outside the window. Sickness rises like
the water to drown us. I push my fist into my mouth
and bite my knuckles. Blackbird wails. Her wings scream
at the criss-cross window. *We have to fly away, fly away, fly home.*

When blackbird thuds down, I suck in breath and hold
my ears to stop the noise. *Mistress is right. We'll have to clip
your black wings. Tame the devil in you.* I lie very still.
It's like a hand is squeezing my head and I can't ever grow.
My cheeks sting and I can't find blackbird. Pain crawls from
chest to belly. I wrap it up, cover it with feathers.

Fifth sitting

Blackbird lives inside me. She teaches me to fly
over the palace gardens. We leave the mistress
sitting on her velvet stool with pink cheeks and
painted lips that never smile. We find black pearls
that are soft and bitter on the tongue.

We lose ourselves in the swish of leaves and
the pearls fall in my hands, bleed on my fingers.
I stand on tiptoe, claw at mama's body, my leg
reaching to get a foothold, to climb up her as if
she is a tree but she is being dragged away, smaller

and smaller until she disappears. Blackbird whirls
in the sky screeching, *We are lost, we are dying!*
Blackbird is captured. Blood stings my lips, pours
from my fists. *Hold her down. Beat her till her feathers fly.
Beat the devil out! Savage! Nothing will tame you!*

I lick blood. Blackbird calls *Mama, Mama,* but I tell her
You have no Mama, you are too wicked.

SENI SENEVIRATNE

After Qana – July 30th 2006

I saw the lunchtime news and now

my arms ache with the dead weight of children whose bodies
one by one, out of the rubble, I have not carried.

My fingers clench against one shoulder and under the bent knees
of a dead girl whose body in pink pyjamas, I have not lifted –

her head thrown back, her eyes closed against the dust –
whose cold hand against my chest, I have not felt.

Despair lands like a bloated pigeon on the acacia tree,
drags down delicate branches, scatters the leaves;

hope disappears over my garden wall like a dragonfly,
as the leaves of the Virginia creeper turn red too soon

and underneath the trellis where the jasmine creeps,
the buddlea drips with purple tears and the butterflies don't care.

Fifty-four civilians, mostly children were killed in an Israeli air-strike on a village in South Lebanon in 2006.

Paths to Freedom
6/6 from a series of paintings **by Fosuwa Andoh**
'Full Moon'

Flags for Freedom
6/6 from a series of batiks **by Oluseyi Ogunjobi**
'Full Moon'

ROMMI SMITH

Full Moon

It is like love, they say; you don't know what it is
until:

that slow moon sinks inside you, deep as realisation.
And just like that moon on night's lips,
its meaning though a statement of itself, is greater
than its circumference. It is understood in phases:
half, full, new; it plays an emotion in you,
you keep trying to set to words.

You could spend your lifetime standing still,
contemplating its existence, comprehending where to find it;
trying to squeeze its definition from the tightest, airless places,
oblivious that you are, at your centre, what it tries to tell you
that you are, eyes turned from its presence in the
smallest acts of kindness.

You don't know what the word is 'til you mourn
its passing; its substance up in flame and you inhaling smoke.
The death of something as routine as Monday;
the thing you never knew you had, yet took
for granted, has you looking for the remnants
of its letters, feeling through the ashes;
the sadness as you're spelling out its ghost.

In exchange for faith, we desire proof's illustration;
to capture it and make it testify to our own narratives,
but in asking a butterfly its destination, we conjure its antithesis.

It is like love, they say; you don't know what it is until
you know: it lives due to love; the bright yolk
held sure in the centre of the shell, not eclipsed, but enclosed;
the moon that sends its mirror upon the tide, the tide
that brings the mirror back. The same moon that lights
the open, terrifying road; the light that urges us:

now walk.

ROMMI SMITH

Tide

(for Ken Saro-Wiwa)

Look, look my friend, over there
how those white sand beaches are
turned by the lap of the tide
into wet black gold by night.

See, my friend, nearer here,
how that flock of gulls
grow fat off Black gold,
gulp the lives out of smaller shells.

One day, we will not be here to witness this;
the lap of that tide will make
each one of us a tenant of its waves.

And only the rocks will testify
to the cackle, overhead, of those
same gulls. Each one, spreading
the long lies of its wings,
writing history out
across the thin blue sky.

FWORDS WRITERS

Tanya Chan-Sam is a South African writer living in Sheffield. She has performed at literature festivals in Sheffield, Cape Town and London. She is a member of Inscribe and was selected for a mentorship award with Apprenticeships in Fiction 2007. Her writing is published in the UK and South Africa. She is published in: *The Invisible Ghetto* (Cosaw, 1993); *Deviant Desire* (Ravan, 1994); *A Woman Sits Down to Write* (Schuster, 2003); *Women Flashing* (Schuster, 2005); *180 Degrees.* (Oshun, 2005); *Tell Tales 2* (Flipped Eye, 2006); *Hair* (Suitcase Press, 2006) and *Sable* (Autumn 2006 and Autumn 2007). Her short story chapbook, *Mr Mohani and Oher Stories* is published by Inscribe/Peepal Tree Press, (2008).

Khadijah Ibrahiim was born in Leeds of Jamaican parentage. Hailed as one of Yorkshire's most prolific poets by BBC Radio, she has appeared alongside the likes of Linton Kwesi Johnson, Lemn Sissay and Benjamin Zephaniah. She is a literary activist, researcher, educator and director of theatre for development and the co-ordinator/mentor for Leeds Young Authors. Her work has appeared in several publications including, *A Journey Through Our History* (The Jamaican Society, 2003), *Voices of Women* (Yorkshire Arts, 2003) and *Hair* (Suitcase Press, 2006). Her poetry chapbook, *Rootz Runnin'* is published by Inscribe/Peepal Tree Press.

Jack Mapanje is a distinguished Malawian poet, linguist, editor and scholar. He has published five books of poetry, *Of Chameleons and Gods*, *The Chattering Wagtails of Mikuyu Prison*, *Skipping Without Ropes*, *The Last of the Sweet Bananas: new and selected poems* and *Beasts of Nalunga,* which won the prestigious Forward Prize for Poetry (2007). He has edited anthologies of poetry and other works including, *Gathering Seaweed: African Prison Writing.* He has written a forthcoming prison memoir, *and crocodiles are hungry at night.* Mapanje is the recipient of numerous literary honours and awards. He is now a senior lecturer in English at Newcastle University, where he teaches creative writing.

Simon Murray (Sy-Mu-Rai) is a poet, writer, artist, and graphic designer of Bajan heritage. His work has appeared in several publications including, *Dance The Guns to Silence: 100 poems for Ken Saro-Wiwa* (Flipped Eye), *Hair* (Suitcase Press); *Toaster for Smoky Laughter* (Inscribe), *SABLE magazine.* He has performed at numerous venues around Britain, at the 2nd International Sable Litfest in the Gambia, and in Barbados as the guest reader at Queen's Park and as a finalist in the Mo Juice Poetry Slam. He is currently working on his first book, *Kill Myself Now* (novel as memoir). A chapbook of the same name, featuring an excerpt from the novel, is published by Inscribe/Peepal Tree Press, (2008).

Seni Seneviratne is a writer, singer, photographer and performer. She was born in Leeds, Yorkshire in 1951 to an English mother and Sri Lankan father. She has been writing poetry since her early teens and was first published in 1989. She has lived in Sheffield since 1978. Her poetry and prose is published in the UK, Denmark, Canada and South Africa. Her debut poetry collection, *Wild Cinnamon and Winter Skin* was published in March 2007 by Peepal Tree Press. She is currently involved in Inscribe, a Northern Black Writers Development Programme and has been accepted on the Complete Works Programme for Black and Asian Writers, supported by Arts Council England, to work on her second collection.

Rommi Smith is a poet and playwright. She has held numerous national and international residencies including Parliamentary Writer in Residence (2007). Her focus was an exploration of the parliamentary act of 1807 to abolish the British Slave Trade. This was the first post of its kind in history. Other residencies include British Council Poet in Residence at California State University in Los Angeles and BBC Writer in Residence for the Commonwealth Games. Her chapbook: *Selected Poems from Mornings and Midnights* was a Poetry Book Society Pamphlet Choice in 2006. The full collection, *Mornings and Midnights* will be published by Peepal Tree Press.

FWORDS VISUAL ARTISTS

Fosuwa Andoh was born in Sheffield and grew up in Sierra Leone, Ghana and The Gambia. She now lives in Leeds. She is an artist, craftsman, educationalist and musician. Her work is inspired by the traditional and visual aesthetics of African's oral tradition, working with various materials including glass, batik and sand. Fosuwa Andoh's work honours the chain of transmission from the ancestors for the creative journey; conveying and maintaining her deep spiritual heritage, producing an immediate and direct communication between viewer and the work. She is presently undertaking research for her Ph.D. at the Prince's School of Traditional Art in London.

Oluseyi (Seyi) Ogunjobi, born in Nigeria, is a storyteller, theatre practitioner, musician, painter, textile artist and translator (Yoruba and Hausa). His paintings have been exhibited across Africa, Europe and America and he has participated in collaborative exhibitions with other African artists at galleries in London. Ogunjobi teaches in schools, colleges and universities, nationally and internationally. Commissions have included work for Harrods, the BBC costume department, The British Museum, and the Victoria & Albert Museum. Ogunjobi is writing a Ph.D. dissertation on the visual languages of the theatre of Duro Ladipo and the Eegun Alare mask performance tradition of the Yoruba people at Leeds University.

LINKS AND SOURCES

www.peepaltreepress.com/fwords
www.myspace.com/fwordscreativefreedom
www.facebook.com/people/FWords_Creative_Freedom/719177992

FWORDS WRITERS' LINKS

JACK MAPANJE
http://www.bloodaxebooks.com/personpage.asp?author=Jack+Mapanje
http://www.contemporarywriters.com/authors/?p=auth02C22P033712627096

SIMON MURRAY
www.symurai.com
www.myspace.com/symurai

SENI SENEVIRATNE
http://www.divacreative.co.uk/seni/
http://www.peepaltreepress.com

ROMMI SMITH
www.rommi-smith.co.uk
www.parliament.uk/slavetrade

SOURCES USED BY WRITERS IN THEIR WORK

Tanya Chan-Sam
'HOW GOD BLESSED AFRICA'

LMS missionaries and religious experiences by J. Cooper
www.unisa.ac.za/contents/publications/docs/KLEI034.pdf

Combating Spiritual and Social Bondage: Early Missions in the Cape Colony by E. Elbourne & R. Ross
https://www.openaccess.leidenuniv.nl/bitstream/1887/4245/1/1246876_084.pdf

A History of Christianity in Africa by Elizabeth Isichei

Religion in Africa – Mission Christianity by Terence Ranger
www.ocms.ac.uk/lectures/

A Concise History of South Africa and *Hoe God Zuid-Afrika Zegende* by Robert Ross

Landscape and Memory by Simon Schama

The Trader, The Owner, The Slave by James Walvin

Simon Murray
'AAAAAAAAAAAAAAAAARGHHHH!'

Grassroots Rising: Cross community Dialogue Facilitation Toolkit – by SAVO, Southwark 2007 And Beyond (a brochure & chronology for anti-slavery resistance timeline).

Do It Yourself – A handbook for changing the world – Pluto Press, 2007 ISBN- 978-0-7453-2637-5 (includes pages of his design work)

Capitalism & Slavery by Eric Eustace Williams

Decolonising the Mind: The Politics of Language in African Literature (Studies in African Literature) by Ngugi Wa Thiong'o

Slaves Who Abolished Slavery: Blacks in Rebellion by Richard Hart

Seni Seneviratne
'SITTING WITH THE MISTRESS'

Amazing Grace: An anthology of poems about slavery 1660-1810 edited by James G. Basker

Ignatius Sancho – An African Man of Letters, National Portrait Gallery publication.

A Short History of Slavery by James Walvin

The Interesting Narrative and other Writings by Olaudah Equiano

Thoughts and Sentiments on the Evils of Slavery by Quobna Ottobah Cugoana

Britain's Slave Empire by James Walvin

The Atlantic Sound by Caryl Phillips

Rommi Smith
'FULL MOON'

Frederick Douglass by Robert Hayden

Taking Off Emily Dickinson's Clothes by Billy Collins

The British Slave Trade: Abolition, Parliament and People by Stephen Farrell, Melanie Unwin and James Walvin